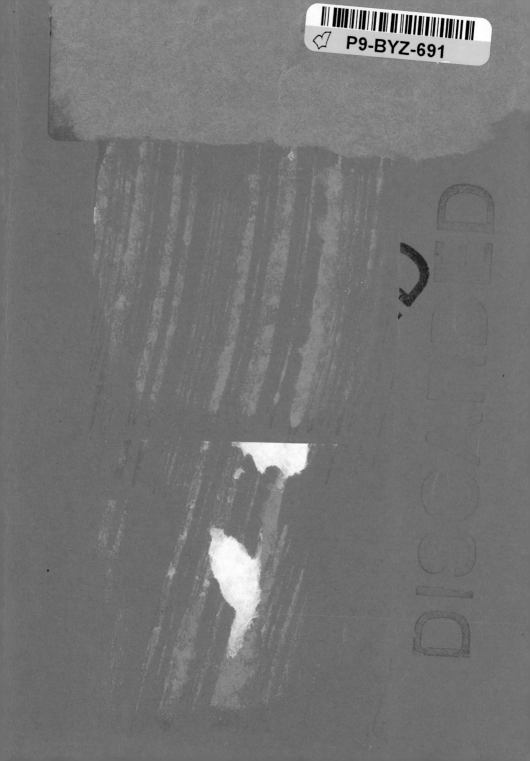

P9-BYZ-691

Who Needs a Bear?

BY BARBARA DILLON
illustrated by Diane deGroat

William Morrow and Company • New York 1981

Printed in the United States of America.
1 2 3 4 5 6 7 8 9 10

Library of Congress Cataloging in Publication Data

Dillon, Barbara.
  Who needs a Bear?
  Summary: A teddy bear, a doll, and a stuffed monkey leave their secure but dull attic, seeking new homes.
  [1. Toys—Fiction] I. De Groat, Diane. II. Title.
P28.9.D54Wh [Fic] 80-26530
ISBN 0-688-00445-8 ISBN 0-688-00446-6 (lib. bdg.)

By the Same Author

The Beast in the Bed
The Good-Guy Cake

For Peter

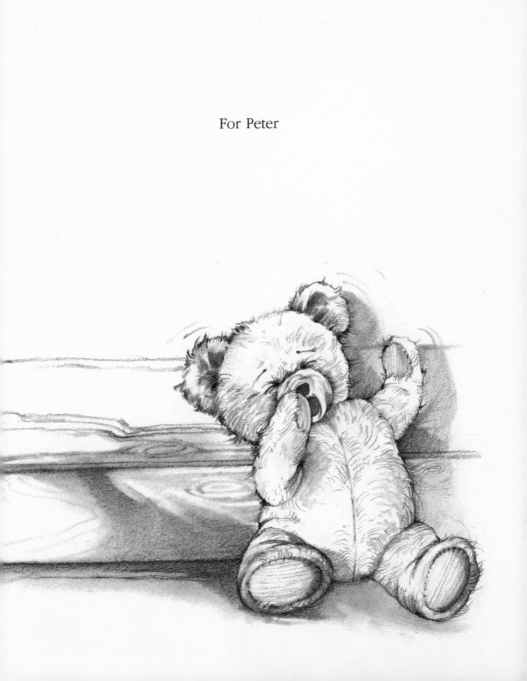

"Up . . . and down . . . and twist . . . around . . ." grunted Malcolm, touching his paws to his toes and then straightening up and pivoting briskly, first to the right and then to the left. Exercising did not come easily to Malcolm, for he was a stout bear and no longer young, and his furry stomach had a tiresome habit of getting in the way when he bent over. But a bear, even a stuffed one, had to keep himself in shape, especially after he had been dumped unceremoniously into a toy box in the attic.

"Up . . . and down . . . and twist . . . around. . . ." gasped Malcolm, anxious to reach his favorite part of the exercise. ". . . twist around, and then sit down." But just as he was about to tell himself to sit, an idea so stupendous, so daring came popping into his head that he said, "Yoicks!" instead and began stumping excitedly about the attic. Clasping and unclasping his paws, he murmured things like, "It's the only answer," and "Why not give it a try?" and "I'm surprised I didn't think of it sooner." And then he said, "I must tell the others at once," and hurried over to the toy box. Inside the box lay Gwendolyn with her eyes closed. Malcolm could tell by the expression on her face she was dreaming of tea parties and doll carriages. Apple, the stuffed monkey, looked as though he might either be remembering fast tricycle rides or thinking up some mischief to get into. Suddenly Gwendolyn's blue eyes opened with a little click, and she tried to sit up.

"Move, you're squishing my knee," she said crossly to Apple. "I'm comfortable where I am," the monkey said through a yawn. "Anyway, you take up too much room in this box."

"I'm telling then," said Gwendolyn. "Malcolm, Apple won't get off my leg."

"Apple," said Malcolm sternly, "please get off Gwendolyn's leg at once. I have something to tell you both."

"Oh, all right," Apple grumbled. But as he rolled toward the corner, he stuck his little red-felt tongue out at the doll. Gwendolyn, with her hard, dimpled fingers, pinched him on the tail.

"I would like to have your attention, please," said Malcolm, clearing his throat importantly. Both Gwendolyn and Apple sat up then and looked respectfully at the bear.

"Just now, as I was quietly doing my exercises," he began, "I—"

"You don't do them so quietly," interrupted Gwendolyn. "You always grunt a lot when you bend down."

"Well, as I was exercising and grunting," said Malcolm, "I was also mulling over some things in my head and—"

"What kind of things?" Apple wanted to know.

"Well, I was thinking that: A., we are not happy here in the attic. B., who would be? C., what shall we do about it?"

"What are the A and B and C for?" Apple asked.

"They are just to help get things going in the right order," Malcolm explained.

"I know what comes after C," said Gwendolyn proudly. "It's D."

"Yes, that's right," said Malcolm, beginning to get muddled. "But let me finish. Where was I?"

"D," said Gwendolyn.

"Oh, yes," said Malcolm. "It was just then that this wonderful idea came to me—right out of the blue." He paused for a moment and looked thoughtfully at Gwendolyn and Apple. "But I guess it really didn't come from out of the blue at all, because blue is outside where the sky is. In here everything is gloomy and shadowy, which is

9

part of the problem, and which is why the idea came to me in the first place."

"What *is* the idea?" Apple demanded impatiently.

"D.," said Malcolm grandly. "We should leave here as soon as possible." He waited for Apple and Gwendolyn to say that of all the ideas they had ever heard, this was certainly the best.

For a moment there was stunned silence in the attic. Then at last Gwendolyn spoke. "But where would we go?" she asked timidly.

"We would go," said Malcolm, "out into the world to find a new home."

"You're kidding!" said Apple.

"The world is awfully big, I think,"said Gwendolyn, trembling at the thought of leaving the attic, which—no matter how dull—was at least familiar and safe.

"Anyway, they might come looking for us one of these days, and then we wouldn't be here," argued Apple, who was also fearful about leaving. But they all knew in their hearts that once a toy is

put in the attic, no one will ever come for it again.

Determinedly Malcolm trotted over to the window. Apple and Gwendolyn scampered after him. Together they peered through the dusty panes to the lawn below.

"It's a long way down," said Gwendolyn, anxiously thinking of her hard, breakable doll's body.

"And if we didn't jump just right, we might end up stuck on the garage roof forever," Apple said worriedly.

"Jumping is the only way," Malcolm told them, suddenly feeling a little scared himself.

"Maybe we ought to think about your plan some more," suggested Apple, feeling so giddy at the prospect of tumbling out of the window that he had to grab hold of the sill.

"I'll jump first to show you how easy it is," Malcolm told them. "Then Apple will be next. Gwendolyn, you can jump on top of us. That way you won't crack anything."

"Thanks a lot, Malcolm," said Apple huffily. "But I happen to be a monkey, not a pillow." He took another quick peek out the window; it really looked awfully nice outside—all sunny and bright and full of things about to burst into bloom.

"Instead of cobwebs and dusty old trunks," said Gwendolyn, looking over his shoulder, "we would be seeing trees and birds and clouds."

"If we did decide to leave," Apple said with a nervous gulp, "when would we go?"

"I was thinking tonight would be a pretty good time," replied Malcolm, trying to sound as if leaving home were nothing so very special.

Gwendolyn looked at Apple and Apple looked at Malcolm, and they all three knew that in that moment the decision to leave home had just been made, and what was more there would be no turning back.

For the rest of the day, the toys bustled about the attic getting ready for their departure. Gwendolyn decided to take a small pink parasol with her. "In case it rains," she explained. "My hair is a mess when it gets wet."

Malcolm rummaged through a carton of old clothes and came up with a snappy green-plaid scarf that he thought looked quite stylish against his white fur. Apple decided to take along a rubber ball that had kept him amused on many a long, boring day. But as he went to retrieve it from in back of a pile of old books, he caught his little red sailor jacket on a nail, making a nasty rip in the sleeve.

"Nobody will want me with a torn coat," he said, his voice trembling.

"Don't worry. I can fix it," Gwendolyn told him. She went quickly to a wicker basket that was her favorite plaything in the attic. Sorting through the spools of thread, she drew out a bright red one and, with Apple in the jacket, managed to sew up the tear so neatly that the sleeve looked as good as new. And she only pricked him twice with the needle, once by mistake and once on purpose.

"I hate her," mumbled Apple, after the second prick. "I hope she breaks a leg when she jumps."

"Of course you don't," Malcolm said reasonably. "Now both of you come help me open the window."

Gwendolyn and Apple ran to the bear's side.

"Oh, look, there's a big moon to light our way," cried Gwendolyn, gazing up at the sky.

"And the stars will help too," said Apple.

"It is a night made for jumping out of windows," agreed Malcolm, hoping the other two wouldn't notice how his paws were shaking.

I can't let them see I'm scared, he thought to himself sternly. I've got to be the leader here, because I'm the biggest and the oldest, and they're depending on me.

"All right," he said aloud, trying to sound cheerful and confident. "You both get on the other side of the window. When I say go, let's all push it as hard as we can. Ready? Go!" Grunting and tugging, the toys managed without too much difficulty to raise the window high enough for them to squeeze through.

Malcolm flicked one end of his scarf over his shoulder and climbed up on the sill. What he had been planning to say was, "This is going to be fun." But what came out was a little high-pitched squeak of terror.

"What did you say?" asked Apple and Gwendolyn together. Malcolm didn't try to speak again.
Instead, he closed his eyes, took a deep breath,
and leaped into the night. The other two, leaning
out as far as they dared, saw him land on his back
in the grass below.

Slowly Malcolm got to his feet and shook himself like a big dog.

"Come on," he called to Apple breathlessly. "Your turn next."

Apple pulled himself miserably up on the windowsill. "I don't think I can do it," he croaked, looking in terror at the ground below.

"Sure you can," said Gwendolyn, and gave him a quick little shove.

"Yikes!" cried Apple, as he somersaulted through the air. "Oh, help! Oh, wow!" And in the next second he landed with a soft thud next to Malcolm. Cautiously he sat up and felt himself all over to be sure he was still in one piece. When he found that he was, he became very brave.

"It was fun," he called up to Gwendolyn. "Don't be scared."

"I'm not," she answered calmly. She put up her parasol and stepped off into space, drifting gracefully down to earth, where she landed neatly beside the monkey. With a businesslike snap, she closed her parasol and hooked it over her arm.

"What happens now?" she asked, gazing out over the wide expanse of lawn in front of them.

In the eerie light of the moon, the lawn looked as distant and cold as the bottom of a pool. Where it sloped into a shadowy line of trees, there was a sudden wild scuttling sound that made all three toys jump in fear.

"What was that?" whispered Apple, grabbing hold of Gwendolyn's parasol.

"Some animal probably," said Malcolm, drawing his scarf more tightly about his throat.

Gwendolyn edged up close to the bear. "We'll all stick together, won't we?" she asked, trying not to sound anxious. Malcolm took her hand comfortingly in his paw, but he made no answer. When he finally did speak, his voice was very quiet. "Suppose," he said, "we weren't always able to stay together."

"Of course we will be able to!" cried Apple.

"Why couldn't we?" demanded Gwendolyn.

"Well, sometimes," said Malcolm, trying to choose his words carefully, "when someone is trying to make a brand-new start, they have to leave a couple of things from their old life behind, even if they may not want to. Sometimes they just have to let go of an old thing before they can get a new one."

Gwendolyn and Apple looked puzzled. "But we can still stay together, can't we?" Gwendolyn asked again.

"We will try," said Malcolm. "But what if we meet a child who wants a doll, but not a monkey or a bear? What then?"

"You mean I would have to go with that child, all by myself?" asked Gwendolyn in dismay.

"Not unless you wanted to," Malcolm told her. "But if you did—"

"I wouldn't," said Gwendolyn.

"We'll see," said Malcolm.

"Come on, let's go," said Apple impatiently.

So the three toys, joining hands and paws, set off bravely across the moonswept lawn.

All night long they trudged from street to street. Gwendolyn got tired and asked Malcolm to carry her parasol. Apple got tired and asked Malcolm to carry his ball. From time to time each of them glanced longingly at the dark, silent houses they passed. They could imagine the sleeping children inside them, nestled all snug in their beds.

"Apple, do you wish you were in one of those nice, warm houses?" Gwendolyn whispered to the monkey once.

"N-no," replied Apple. "It's more fun out here in the d-dark." And he grabbed Gwendolyn's hand as a big raccoon suddenly lumbered into their path.

"Beware the dog," said the raccoon, peering at them through his little black mask. "He has teeth like knives and could tear you to pieces."

"Oh, I wish we had never left home," wailed Gwendolyn, already imagining her white pinafore ripped to shreds.

"We'll just have to be very careful," said Malcolm, glancing quickly over his shoulder. "In the dark, we are not easy to see, and we don't have

the kind of smell that makes dogs wild and crazy.
We'll be all right."

"What are you doing out at night, anyway?"
asked the raccoon. "Searching for mice? Looking
for berries?"

"Looking for a new home," explained Apple. "Do you happen to know where any are?"

"If I were you, I'd try the park," advised the raccoon, sitting down to scratch his ear. "It's full of hollow logs and stumps and trees, all good places for dens. And there's plenty to eat there too—birds' eggs and grasshoppers and seeds and a duck pond full of frogs and goldfish."

"Yuck," said Gwendolyn.

"Where is the park?" Malcolm asked, a sudden memory stirring in his head. Years ago, as a young bear, he had been taken to a wonderful place with trees and a pond in it and a playground filled with children.

"Go straight down this road," the raccoon told them. "Take a left, go one more block, and take a right, and you'll come to the park entrance."

"Thank you for your help," said Malcolm. "Let's go," he said to Gwendolyn and Apple, who were already skipping on ahead of him.

"Don't forget about the dog!" the raccoon called after them.

The moon was fading into a thin white wafer as the three friends scurried along. And in the east the sky began to take on a pearly hue.

All at once the toys saw up ahead of them the dim, shaggy shape of a big animal. He was standing stock-still, with one front paw slightly raised, and in the next moment he was bounding toward them, filling the quiet dawn with ferocious barks. Gwendolyn screamed and grabbed Apple, who was too scared to do anything but grab Malcolm. As there was no one for Malcolm to grab, he did the next best thing—he growled. Though because he hadn't used his growl in a long while, it sounded a little tinny. Nevertheless, the dog skidded to a surprised stop, stared at the toys, and turned his barks into threatening snarls.

He is very bouncy, and his paws seem too big for the rest of him, Malcolm thought. He is probably just a puppy. But that doesn't mean his teeth aren't sharp as nails.

Then the dog began charging wildly toward them again. "I'm going to rough you funny-

looking people up," he announced gaily, as he
thundered into their path.

Thinking fast, Malcolm turned and quickly
threw Apple's ball in the direction from which
they had just come. The dog gave a gleeful bark
and bounced after it, losing interest, at least for

the moment, in his intended victims. The toys
had no intention of waiting for the dog to come
bouncing back with the ball in his teeth. They
took to their heels and ran for dear life.

"We make a left here," panted Malcolm, as they
reached the end of the road.

"And here we go right," said Apple several yards farther on.

"Oh, I can see the park now,"cried Gwendolyn. "Ooh, it looks beautiful!"

Up to the entrance and through the gates the three jogged, and a second later flung themselves down under the protecting branches of a big maple tree. The night had been a long, hard one, and they were all glad to rest for a while—even Apple, whose favorite thing was definitely not resting.

In the early-morning light, the trees with their tender new spring leaves looked as if they were wrapped in green tissue paper. A robin, out for an early breakfast, eyed the toys inquisitively as he pulled a long worm from the soft damp earth. The park was very quiet and very peaceful.

"Where are all the children?" Gwendolyn asked, leaning against Malcolm's shoulder. "I thought you said there'd be lots and lots in the park."

"They'll come out later," Malcolm told her, "when the sun gets higher in the sky." And he realized in surprise that he was glad there were no children around; for the moment, he was quite content just to sit and gaze peacefully up at the soft blue sky.

Slowly the park began to come to life. Joggers in brightly colored warm-up suits, looking neither to the right nor the left, passed close by the toys without noticing them. A couple of bike riders wheeled past next, their eyes fixed steadily on the path ahead.

The first one to discover the toys' presence was a timid Scotty on a leash, who gave one fierce bark before rushing to hide behind the legs of her mistress.

"What did you see, Jill? A rabbit?" asked the lady she was with. But in the second before the woman glanced over in the toys' direction, Malcolm and Gwendolyn and Apple had whisked out of sight behind the maple's sturdy trunk.

"Silly doggie," said Jill's mistress. "Sweet, silly, little doggie." And she pulled her pet along the path toward a bench in the sun.

Several mothers pushing carriages strolled past, followed by a father and his two sons carrying a bag of stale bread for the ducks.

Apple simply could not hold still another moment.

"How long are we going to stay here?" he grumbled. "I wish I had my ball." And because he had nothing better to do, he gave one of Gwendolyn's curls a sly yank. Gwendolyn squealed and tried to nip him on the tail with her pearly little teeth. Malcolm could see the time had come to get moving.

"We'll go look for the playground," he said, hauling himself to his feet. "I'll lead the way. You two stay *right* in back of me and *no* monkeyshines. Do you understand, Apple? Do you understand, Gwendolyn?"

The three toys set off across the park, keeping

close to trees, skittering under hedges, jumping behind bushes if they thought someone was looking their way. The sound of children's voices, laughing and shouting in the distance, guided them around the duck pond, past a rose garden, in back of a row of cherry trees, and finally to a place enclosed by a stone wall with a sign over the entrance gate that said *Dragon Pit.* Inside the wall was a long log in the shape of a dragon on which several children were climbing. Next to it were seesaws, and beyond the seesaws were swings and a slide, and on all of them, just as Malcolm had remembered, were children.

Right outside the wall was a large forsythia bush in bloom. Malcolm stepped quickly behind it, pulling Gwendolyn and Apple down next to him.

"We don't want just anyone to discover us," he explained. "We have to be very careful."

"I would like to try one of those swings shaped like a little chair," said Gwendolyn, peering longingly through the branches of the forsythia.

"They're only for babies," scoffed Apple. "I'd like to climb to the top of that big slide."

"You'd get all dizzy and scared if you did," Gwendolyn said with a laugh.

At that moment, a girl carrying a doll with curly blond hair entered the Dragon Pit.

"Wait here, Alice," she said, setting the doll down on a bench near the forsythia bush. Unwinding a skip rope from around her waist, the girl began to jump in slow circles and recite in a singsong voice:

> I had a little monkey,
> I sent him to the country.
> I fed him on gingerbread.
> He jumped out the winder,
> And broke his little finger,
> And now my monkey's dead.

"Ugh, what an awful song!" Apple shuddered and clapped his paws over his ears as she began to chant the rhyme again.

But Gwendolyn thought the girl was wonderful. She was also interested in Alice, sitting by
herself on the bench. Eagerly she turned to Malcolm. "Could I go say hello?" she asked.

Malcolm looked hard at the doll and at the
jump roper and then at Gwendolyn.

"Yes, that might be a good idea," he said
slowly. All at once he put his furry arms around
Gwendolyn and gave her a big bear hug.

"Go quickly, while the jump roper has her
back turned," he said.

Swift and quiet as a mouse, Gwendolyn stepped from in back of the forsythia, darted to the
bench, and quickly shinnied up the leg.

"Hello, I'm Gwendolyn," she said to the surprised doll sitting there. Although Gwendolyn
had a rather shrill little voice, no one heard it but
Alice, Malcolm, and Apple, for people can't hear
toys talk.

Alice stared coldly at Gwendolyn. "How come
you're out by yourself and your dress is dirty?"
she asked.

"I'm not by myself. I'm with Malcolm and Apple," Gwendolyn told her. "And my dress is not dirty."

"It is too, and so are your socks," said Alice.

"You're rude," said Gwendolyn, and gave the other doll a shove. Alice did a stiff-legged somersault in the air and landed on her head under the bench. Gwendolyn had not meant to push her so hard.

"Ooh, I'm sorry," she said, jumping down beside her. "Here, let me help you up."

Ruefully Alice examined a smudge on her skirt. "Boy, you can push hard," she said. But her voice sounded more respectful than angry.

At that moment the jump roper, who had jumped to the seesaws and back without once catching her foot in the rope, came toward the bench.

"Where did you come from?" she said, staring at Gwendolyn. "And how did you get on the ground, Alice?" The girl slung her jump rope over her shoulder and picked both dolls up.

"You're really cute." She smiled and pushed back a strand of hair from Gwendolyn's cheek. Gwendolyn, entranced, smiled back. How lovely it was to be held by a little girl again! The girl looked slowly around the Dragon Pit.

"I'm afraid you've been left behind," she said to Gwendolyn in a pleased voice. "But don't worry. You can come home with Alice and me."

At that moment Gwendolyn suddenly remembered the others. "But I can't leave without my friends!" she cried. "We have to stick together, Malcolm and Apple and me."

"Which one is that bear hiding behind the yellow bush?" asked Alice.

"That's Malcolm. Malcolm, help!" wailed Gwendolyn, as she was hoisted to the girl's shoulder.

"We don't need another Teddy," Alice told her. "We already have one at home, and he's a big grouch."

Gwendolyn only wailed louder as she was carried through the gate of the Dragon Pit.

Alice tried to comfort her new friend. "At home we have tea parties," she yelled, trying to make herself heard above Gwendolyn's wails.

"With real cupcakes. We get to watch television and go to the grocery store, and when we're alone we can go hopping around and knock the furniture out of the dollhouse and turn on the water in the bathroom. It'll be fun."

Still Gwendolyn wept, but not quite so loudly. "What kind of icing on the cupcakes?" she said, sniffling.

"Chocolate"—Alice smiled—"with colored sprinkles."

Malcolm, who had scrambled to his feet in dismay as Gwendolyn was whisked past him, now stood on tiptoe to get the last possible glimpse of her as she disappeared around a bend.

"It was too quick," he cried in a choked voice. "I wasn't ready to have her go so soon." And he began to think of all the things he should have reminded her about—like not pinching or biting when she was angry and remembering to say please and thank you. Now it was too late. She'd just have to manage on her own.

With a heavy heart, Malcolm picked up Gwendolyn's parasol, which lay on the ground at his feet, and hooked it over his arm. Good-byes are terrible, he thought. Hellos are so much nicer. Then all at once he noticed with alarm that Apple had disappeared, and he had absolutely no idea what had become of him. He ducked out from under the forsythia bush and headed back at a rapid trot along the way they had come from the entrance of the park.

"Apple!" he called anxiously. "Where are you?" But his question was greeted with silence. "Apple!" he called again. Still no answer. Quickly Malcolm transferred Gwendolyn's parasol to his mouth and dropped down on all fours, which was the way he walked when he really wanted to make time.

"I should never have let that monkey out of my sight," he fumed, pushing through hedges and bushes. Ahead lay the duck pond, and as Malcolm crept up to its banks, he had a sudden terrible thought. Supposing Apple had fallen in and was even now floating helplessly on his back. In

dread Malcolm squinted out over the water's glinting blue surface. He saw a number of toy sailboats bobbing up and down, but no monkey. Then suddenly from the top of the willow under which he was standing came a thin, little cry for help. Shading his eyes with a paw, Malcolm peered into the branches. High above his head he could just make out a small spot of red.

"I climbed up here so that awful girl wouldn't get me," wailed the spot, "and now I can't get down."

"Hold tight and come down backwards," Malcolm advised. "I'll be here to catch you." But Apple had gotten himself stuck out on the end of a limb and was too terrified to move.

Maybe I'd better go up after him, thought Malcolm. But he jumped in back of the willow instead as a man, followed by a boy carrying a sailboat, came walking toward him.

"I know you're disappointed, Rob," the man was saying. "But after all, a sailboat is a great birthday present."

"I like monkeys better, Dad," said Rob. "Aunt Janet said she was sending a monkey." And he handed the boat to his father and began walking on all fours, stopping every once in a while to scratch himself and make chattering sounds.

"I am a woolly monkey," he announced, as he came to the tree in which Apple was hanging. "And I am an expert climber." He looked up into the leafy branches of the willow and saw the sleeve of Apple's red jacket.

"Something's stuck up there," he said. "Maybe it's an apple."

"Wrong kind of tree and wrong time of year for fruit," said the father.

Suddenly Rob's eyes widened with surprise. "I think it's a monkey tree," he said. "That looks like the arm of a monkey."

His father sighed. He was getting tired of hearing about monkeys. But he put down the sailboat and gave the willow a good shake. Apple held on for dear life. The father shook the tree again. Apple lost his grip and came plopping down through the branches. He landed with a thud right at Rob's feet.

"I don't believe it. It *is* a monkey," said the father, laughing.

For a moment, Rob was too overcome to say anything at all. He picked Apple up and just grinned at him.

"You're a wild one, I can tell," he said, looking with approval into Apple's shiny brown eyes. Apple gazed back. It was a case of love at first sight. But then Apple thought about Malcolm. Eagerly he peered over Rob's shoulder, searching for the bear.

"I will call you Apple because that is what you looked like hanging up there in the branches," Rob was saying. But Apple scarcely heard him, for he had caught sight of Malcolm standing behind the willow.

"You and Gwendolyn come with us," he cried. "This boy really seems nice."

Maybe I should join them, thought Malcolm. I could just pretend that the wind had blown me down from a lower limb which they hadn't happened to notice a bear was sitting on. But then as he watched Rob hugging Apple he suddenly realized how young they both were.

"They belong together," he said to himself. "Anyone can see that. They don't need a third party hanging around."

There was only one thing to do, and Malcolm did it. Trying to look especially cheerful, he raised one paw and bravely waved good-bye. It wasn't easy, for acting especially cheerful when you are especially sad is a very hard thing to do, as anyone knows who has tried it.

Malcolm kept on waving till Apple's head, jiggling up and down on Rob's shoulder as the boy skipped away down the path, looked no bigger than a marble.

When at last both boy and monkey had disappeared from sight, Malcolm turned with a sigh and sat down under the willow to rest and to think, somewhat glumly, about his own future.

The park seemed very lonely with both Gwendolyn and Apple gone. And how strange it was, after all this time, suddenly to have no one depending on him anymore, strange and a little scary. So to bolster his courage, Malcolm began talking out loud, taking comfort from the sound of his own gruff voice.

"The problem is," he told himself, "who needs a bear anyway? Someone must, I'm sure. It's just a matter of finding them." He paused for a moment, his forehead furrowed in thought. "So I could: A., sit here and wait for a finder to come along. B., become that finder myself and move on to another part of the park."

And in the middle of trying to decide whether

he should try Plan A or Plan B, his head dropped down on his chest, and he drifted off to sleep. He dreamed that Apple went rolling past in a baby stroller, holding Gwendolyn's parasol over his head. He dreamed Gwendolyn was skipping rope on the branch of a tree blooming with big red rubber balls. All at once he awoke with a start as he felt himself being whisked off the ground. In alarm, he looked up to see a freckle-faced boy grinning at him. Next to the boy stood his two friends, and Malcolm knew right away from the queasy feeling in his stomach that none of them were up to any good.

"Hey, look at this crazy bear," said the one holding him.

"He's got a scarf and an umbrella," cried a red-haired one. "Neato."

"What a bear! What a bear!" said the third, who was wearing a T-shirt that had *Tough Stuff* written across the chest. And he grabbed Malcolm from his friend and kicked the bear off the end of his

toe like a football. The other two laughed as Malcolm went sailing in one direction and Gwendolyn's parasol in the other.

Oh-oh, I'm in big trouble, thought Malcolm, as the sky and the ground went spinning crazily past him.

The boy with freckles picked him up from the ground and pitched him to his red-headed buddy. "Let's make him our mascot," he suggested. And the three went running across the park to the ball field, tossing Malcolm back and forth between them.

"Hey, Meehan, what've you got there?" a big boy in a baseball cap asked, as the younger boys headed toward some bleachers. He looked closer at Malcolm and gave a loud guffaw. "You've got a Teddy bear," he said mockingly. "Little Tommy Meehan brought his Teddy bear to the park. Isn't that cute?"

"I did not," said the red-haired boy defensively. "We just found the thing sitting under a tree." To prove that he had absolutely no need of stuffed animals, he took Malcolm by the leg and pitched him carelessly toward a nearby bench, where the bear landed with a dull thud against the hard slats of the seat. Bruised and indignant from his mauling, Malcolm lay on his back, panting heavily, but grateful to have escaped from his tormentors.

If that's what being a mascot is like, no thank you, he thought. I was lucky not to have had an arm or a leg pulled off. Warily turning his head, he saw with relief that the boys were already clambering up to the top of the empty bleachers. Apparently they had forgotten about him, at least for the moment. Quickly he began easing himself toward the edge of the bench until he was able to roll off the seat onto the ground. Then, bit by bit, he inched his way on his belly to the safety of a big hedge, just as he had once seen a commando do on television.

For a long time he lay huddled beneath the hedge, afraid to venture out from under its branches lest he be seen by the boys again or perhaps by someone even worse. Gradually the air became cooler, and the sky turned the color of pink applesauce as the setting sun slipped lazily behind a line of trees.

"Well, I can't stay here forever," Malcolm told himself, feeling the ground growing cold beneath him. He sat up and cautiously stuck his head out from the shrubbery. The boys had disappeared, and the park was deserted and silent except for the sleepy twitter of birds flying home to their nests. Malcolm was not happy at the thought of spending the night outdoors all alone. He wasn't afraid exactly, but as darkness fell the trees began to look funny to him, more like huge animals and hovering giants than maples and oaks and willows. And he couldn't help noticing when he stepped all the way out of the shrubbery that odd shadows lurked just beyond the glow of the park lights, which came on as the last rays of the sun faded from the sky.

Suddenly from out of one of those gloomy patches loomed a hunched shape.

"Hey, Boss, where'd you get that groovy scarf?" a hoarse voice inquired, as a good-sized rat appeared on the path directly in front of him. "I could use a scarf like that. Whaddya want for it?"

"My scarf doesn't happen to be for sale," Malcolm told him, nervously eyeing the rat's long, chisellike teeth.

"Everything's got a price," said the rat with a laugh. He moved closer to Malcolm, staring up at him with eyes that looked like wet, black beads.

"How about coming down to my place?" he suggested. "I have stuff there you'd be crazy about. Nails and nuts, cans and coins, buckles and beads. I'm sure we could work out a nice little trade. The beads are really something, made from colored glass."

But Malcolm shook his head. "I don't want buckles and beads," he said. "I want my scarf." And he tried to step past the rat.

"Not so fast, Fatso," rasped the rat. "I want that scarf, and I'm going to get it one way or another." His little eyes glinted in the dark, and although he hadn't made a move, Malcolm had the uncomfortable feeling that the crouching rat was poised like a spring, ready to uncoil at any moment.

"Are you going to hand it over peacefully, or do I have to use persuasion?" the rat croaked. "Maybe you'd like to have your ears gnawed or the end of your nose whittled down a little."

"It's my scarf, and I'm keeping it," Malcolm said stubbornly, though his knees felt weak with fright.

What happened next came about so swiftly and so silently that neither the bear nor the rat had time to do anything but grunt and squeak in surprise.

From out of the dark, sleek and swift as a jaguar, pounced a big black cat. Malcolm stood rooted, too startled to do anything but stare in horror. The cat quickly and deftly pinned the frantic rat beneath her front paws. The rat's tail thrashed in mad circles as he tried to escape from his attacker.

"Oh, this is terrible!" cried Malcolm, covering

his eyes with his paws. Then he turned and lumbered across the park as fast as he could go, the rat's desperate squeal of "Oh, no, oh no!" ringing in his ears.

Past the duck pond he fled and past the Dragon Pit and the rose garden.

"That rat's probably dead as a doornail by now," he said to himself, as he came to the maple tree under which he and Gwendolyn and Apple had sat together that morning. "But who's complaining? If it hadn't been for that cat, my stuffing might have been strewn over the whole park."

Up ahead were the entrance gates, and Malcolm hurried toward them in relief.

When he was safely outside the park, he slumped down against a fire hydrant to rest and give his knees a chance to stop shaking. Never in his life had he had such a wild, action-packed day.

Across the street he could see a neat row of houses; each of them looked warm and safe and inviting. Surely, Malcolm thought, there must be somebody in one of them who would take in a stray bear. The question was, which one?

Malcolm waited till there were no cars coming. Then he stepped onto the curb, remembering to look both ways, and hurried across to the other side.

Directly in front of him was a square brick house. He looked thoughtfully at its lighted windows and then at the white shingled house on its right. He looked at the gray stone one on the left. He glanced up at the sky and saw one bright star shining. Quickly he made a wish. "Let me choose the right house," he whispered. Just to be on the safe side, he added, "Eeny meeny, miney mo, my mother told me to pick this one." His paw pointed to the brick house in front of him, which for some reason was the one he had planned to try all along. Without further ado, he stumped up the front steps and sat down on the doormat next to a folded newspaper. He didn't have long to wait. In a few minutes, the front door opened, and a woman stepped out on the porch. When she saw Malcolm, she burst out laughing.

"Are you the new paper boy?" she asked, picking him up to get a better look. She glanced curiously up and down the street.

"Who could have left you here?" she wondered. "Someone, I guess, who knows how nutty

I am about bears." She tucked the folded newspaper under one arm and Malcolm under the other and went into the house. She put the paper on the hall table and carried Malcolm up the stairs.

"You're a wonderful bear," she said, cuddling him in her arms. "I'm so glad you've come. Even though there are no children here, I think you'll be very happy with us. Let me introduce you to the others."

She opened a door at the end of the hall and switched on a light.

"Surprise, everyone," she said. "Welcome a new member into our family."

Malcolm could see a big bed on which sat lots of other bears—brown, yellow, black, and one or two white ones. In a rocking chair sat three more. On the night table was a yellow one in track shorts and roller skates. On top of a chest were twin gray ones. On a bureau stood a tiny bear in a yellow hat. Malcolm noticed that some of the bears were old, with worn patches in their fur.

"I'll leave you to get acquainted," said the woman, setting Malcolm gently down on the bed. Then she turned out the light and went downstairs.

Anyone standing outside the door would have

heard quite a lot of thumping and scuffling going on. That was Malcolm and the others cuffing each other softly, which is the way bears—at least stuffed ones—get acquainted. The little bear in the yellow hat was particularly interested in Malcolm.

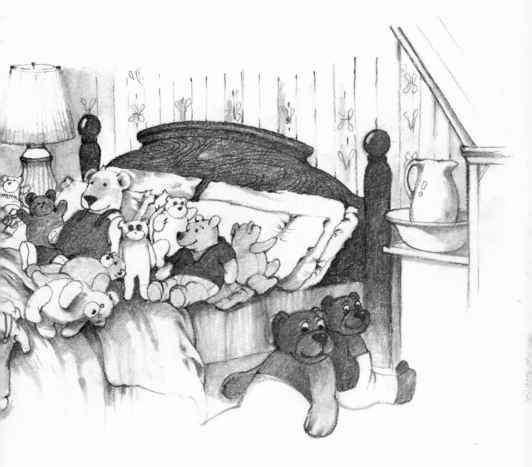

He climbed up on his shoulder and peered in his ears and felt his round, black nose.

"Do you know any good stories?" he asked. "We all love stories."

So Malcolm told the bears about his adven-

tures, from jumping out of the attic window to his arrival on the porch below. And the bears said "Amazing!"and "Imagine that!" and "How awful!" in all the right places.

When bedtime came, the little bear took off his yellow hat and snuggled up against Malcolm for the night. "Tell again about the monkey," he said sleepily, "and how he got stuck in the tree."

Malcolm soon grew to love the big, sunny bedroom that he shared with the other bears. It was a very peaceful, sociable place. When he and his friends got tired of talking and napping, they wrestled quietly with one another or climbed up on the windowsill to see what was going on in the park across the way. Sometimes at night they sneaked into the kitchen looking for honey. The woman with whom they lived never understood how their paws got so sticky.

Malcolm felt sure that Gwendolyn was going to many tea parties. He imagined Apple was having a happy, rough-and-tumble time with Rob. He

was glad for them both. But, as for himself, parties and roughhousing were all well and good,
but when you got to be a senior bear, a bear who
had been through thick and thin, a soft bed and
good friends were best.

Dillon, Barbara
Who Needs a Bear?

DATE DUE	BORROWER'S NAME